Rosalie's
Catastrophes

Merry Christmas
From
Grandma

Rosalie's
Catastrophes

Ginette Anfousse

Illustrated by Marisol Sarrazin
Translated by Linda Gaboriau

RAGWEED
THE ISLAND PUBLISHER

Originally published in French as *Les catastrophes de Rosalie*
by Ginette Anfousse, (Les éditions la courte échelle inc.,
1987).

Cover and book illustrations: Marisol Sarrazin
Printed and bound in Canada by: Webcom

*Ragweed Press acknowledges the generous support of the Canada
Council.*

Published by:
Ragweed Press
P.O. Box 2023
Charlottetown, P.E.I.
Canada, C1A 7N7

Canadian Cataloguing in Publication Data
Anfousse, Ginette, 1944-

[Catastrophes de Rosalie. English]

Rosalie's catastrophes

Translation of: Les catastrophes de Rosalie.
ISBN 0-921556-47-0 (pbk). — ISBN 0-921556-49-7 (bound)

I. Sarrazin, Marisol, 1965-   II. Title.   III. Title:
Catastrophes de Rosalie. English.

PS8551.N42C3713 1994   jC843'.54   C94-950178-6
PZ7. A64Ro 1994

For Fernande, my mother,
with much love and admiration.

Contents

Prologue

Now I don't want you to think that I say "Holy hopping horrors" because I'm badly brought up. I say it because it annoys my mothers. Actually, it drives all seven of them crazy. I like teasing them once in a while, they're so perfect.

I am exactly nine years, seven months and three days old and my name is Rosalie. My life began with a catastrophe, one holy hopping horror of an enormous catastrophe.

First of all, I was only two months old when I lost my real mother and father. They died in the worst airplane crash in the history of Quebec. I was too little to be sad. The only souvenir I have of my parents is a colour photograph where I'm squeezed in between them, chewing on a pacifier and crying my head off.

That was when my father's seven sisters adopted me. I promptly inherited a whole litany of nicknames. Even today, I'm more than just plain old Rosalie. I'm also: Aunt Alice's chickadee, Aunt Beatrice's loveheart, Aunt Colette's sweetness, Aunt Diane's angel, Aunt Elisabeth's cockatoo, Aunt Florence's ladybug and Aunt Gertrude's monster.

For the past nine years, five months and three days we have been living together in the house on St. Joseph Boulevard. It's a huge two-storey house, just across the street from Saint Mary's Church. My seven aunts have lots of respect for this fine old boulevard, but I prefer the little side streets myself. That's where I grew up, along with my friends, in the alleys and garages well out of my mothers' sight.

Aunt Alice, my oldest aunt, is really gentle. Too gentle, as my Aunt Beatrice always says, to run a household.

Aunt Beatrice is not at all gentle. She's as long and skinny as a celery stalk and she's always waving her arms and hands. She reminds me of a traffic cop. She also has sharp grey eyes that never miss a thing. Eyes that notice the tiniest speck of dust, the tiniest thing left lying around.

She's in charge of the pantry and she's always on the lookout for waste. Aunt Beatrice supervises everyone's comings and goings. She's like the guardian of all doors, stairs and hallways.

That's why I've given her a secret nickname:
Sergeant Celery.

The day we arrived on St. Joseph Boulevard,
Aunt Beatrice took charge of the household in
general and, more specifically, of my education.
Under the watchful eye of Sergeant Celery, I,
baby Rosalie, didn't play pattycake with my
mashed potatoes for long.

I didn't get to spit many mouthfuls of green peas on her spotless floors. But I did, on the other hand, swallow an unbelievable quantity of pureed carrots, mountains of spinach, truckloads of vitamin C and barrels of codliver oil.

For the sake of my health, Aunt Beatrice calculated everything: protein, calories, the carbo-whatchamacallits ... And with just as much precision, she kept track of my sleeping and waking hours.

And even now, at nine and a half, I am still the victim of her holy hopping horror of a balanced diet and regular routine.

Every night, at nine o'clock sharp, as soon as I've drunk my obligatory three gulps of water, Aunt Beatrice takes me up to my room. "Did you brush your teeth properly, loveheart?" she asks me as she tucks in my quilt. She fluffs up my pillow, pushes aside my teddybear and kisses me on the forehead. Then, triumphant, she leaves my room. And I lie there in the dark, waiting ...

First I wait for Aunt Alice to arrive with her two molasses cookies. Then for Aunt Colette to appear with her slice of melt-in-your-mouth orange cheese. Then, I wait for

Aunt Diane's candied fig, Aunt Elisabeth's handful of cherries, Aunt Florence's chewy caramel, and, for the final touch, Aunt Gertrude's glass of chocolate milk.

Then, and only then, can I fall asleep.

Not one of my aunts is aware of the others' visits, so there, in the secrecy of my room, far from Sergeant Celery's watchful eye, I silently take advantage of the situation.

• • • •

Last week I found out why Aunt Beatrice had been following me around and sighing. She'd pinch my cheeks and pat my tummy and sigh some more. She was obviously not very happy. Finally, she let the cat out of the bag.

"I don't understand, loveheart, I just don't understand! You should have lost your baby fat ages ago! Are you absolutely sure you don't stuff yourself with sweets and junk at school or when I'm not looking?"

Aunt Alice replied, "You always exaggerate. The child is the picture of health. Don't tell me you want to starve my chickadee and put her on a diet." Gentle Aunt Alice was so offended that Aunt Beatrice didn't dare say another word.

Then, because of my own stupidity, because of my own holy horrible absent-mindedness, a few days later, Aunt Beatrice figured everything out.

I love food, so I must have been pretty preoccupied when I left my lunch bag on the kitchen counter that morning. Finally, at noontime, after searching through my locker, my desk and my schoolbag, I accepted the fact that poor little Rosalie had absolutely nothing for lunch.

I sat down in a corner of the cafeteria and I announced loudly, "I don't think I'm very hungry today."

Nicolas, a tall, skinny sixth-grader, laughed and joked, "Did you hear that? Rosalie-the-pumpkin is going on a diet."

I could have bitten his ears off, but I was so embarrassed, I just lowered my head and studied the linoleum.

Black-and-white linoleum isn't that interesting but it took my mind off my problem. Suddenly, two high-heeled red shoes stopped right in front of me. I raised my head. There was the principal. She put seven plump little lunchbags down on the table and said, "This is for you, Rosalie, but don't ask me why. They kept arriving one after the other."

I understood immediately. On each bag, there was a little note scribbled in pencil. Basically, it read:

"This time, I forgive you for being so absent-minded. Don't tell your aunts. It's our little secret. Enjoy your lunch!"

One of the bags was signed Alice, another Beatrice, another Colette, another Diane, another Elisabeth, another Florence and the last one Gertrude.

I just smiled foolishly and muttered, "What a holy hopping horror of a holy hopping horrible mess!"

I was really fed up. Especially since the skinny sixth-grader was already pointing at my lunch bags, laughing and shouting, "Did you see that? Did you see that? Look at Rosalie-the-pumpkin's seven diets!"

I could hardly swallow a piece of orange. Later that afternoon, I took the seven lunch bags with their scribbled notes home with me. I lined them up in full view on the kitchen counter. It was the only way I could make my aunts understand that seven lunches was going a bit too far.

That evening, Aunt Beatrice called the first real family council. My six aunts admitted everything to Sergeant Celery. Everything — the molasses cookies, the slices of orange cheese, the candied figs, the handfuls of cherries, the chewy caramels and the large glasses of chocolate milk. I know because I heard everything … through the keyhole.

After each confession, Aunt Beatrice let out a little cry, a long sigh, then another little cry. She was evaluating the extent of the betrayal.

Then my aunts whispered for the longest while. Since I could no longer hear a thing, I crept up to my room. The following morning, the council decreed: I had to go on a diet and lose all those proteins, calories and carbo-whatchamacallits. I also had to:

go swimming with Aunt Beatrice on Mondays,

go to a fitness class with Aunt Colette on Tuesdays,

go for a walk on the mountain with Aunt Diane on Wednesdays,

go to a judo class with Aunt Elisabeth on Thursdays,

go to a yoga class with Aunt Florence on Fridays,

and go running with Aunt Gertrude on Saturdays.

Aunt Alice was in charge of Sundays. She kindly suggested that it could be my day to rest.

Now, at night, after my three obligatory gulps of water, Aunt Alice is the only one who slips into my room in the dark. A bit ashamed, she still leaves two big molasses cookies under my pillow.

A month later, Aunt Beatrice was in a good mood again and I had lost at least two kilos. I gathered my seven aunts together in the living room and, standing on the scales, I decided to speak my mind.

"I know that all the mothers in the world only want what's best for their children." (I looked Aunt Beatrice straight in the eye.) "I know it's possible for a mother to have seven children." (And I looked at each of my aunts, one after another.) "But, how can I say it … it's quite rare, and very difficult, for a single child to have seven mothers at the same time."

Pause. I looked up at the ceiling. Then, I continued.

"Most of all, it's … it's really exhausting!"

At that point, I think I examined my shoes. And since I couldn't think of anything else to say, Aunt Alice, gentle Aunt Alice, came up to me. She stroked my cheeks and murmured, "My chickadee has lost her rosy baby complexion. She doesn't look well, don't you agree?"

Sergeant Celery shrugged her shoulders and sighed.

And all my aunts, without exception, decided that the great exercise program could be discontinued.

Aunt Elisabeth was particularly relieved because she was always afraid my studies were being neglected. Personally, I thought it was my friends who had been neglected.

At last, I would be able to see my friend Julie whenever I wanted. That meant at school, because we're in the same class, and after school, because she lives next door.

Julie is my best friend. We're always together. She can add, subtract, multiply and divide as fast as any electronic calculator. She's at the top of the class in math. Not me. I'm not at the top of the class in anything. My worst subject is spelling. But it doesn't really matter, because, personally, I'd rather talk than write. Talking is much faster and no one, absolutely no one, can guess how many spelling mistakes I'm capable of making.

Miss LaFrance, my French teacher, doesn't agree. She says it's just as important to know how to write as it is to know how to talk.

Last week she came up with what she thought was a great idea. Everyone had to choose a subject. Then at home, we had to jot down all our good ideas. She said that was called an outline. She claimed an outline would help us the next day, when each one of us would have to stand up in front of the class and talk about our subject for ten minutes.

Personally, I didn't think it was such a great idea. Julie didn't either. Talking for ten minutes was no problem. But having to choose a subject, develop an outline, and write it down was the worst holy hopping horror of a home-work assignment I'd ever had.

I racked my brains for the longest time. Then, suddenly, looking at the old photograph where I'm snuggled between my parents and chewing on my pacifier, I thought of my subject. First I wrote my title in capital letters in the middle of the page, and then I continued:

THE ORFAN

I have no father and no mother. Its a terrible trageday and I shoudn't be here at all. I shoud be in a big orfanage with other boy and girl orfans like me. Much to my despear, my fathers seven sisters decided to adopt me. And thats why today I find myself an only child. Its just not fair cause my seven aunts decided to be like seven mothers to me. First of all, Aunt Alice is always checking to make sure my nose isnt running like a babies. Or to make sure I ate enuff.

Aunt Beatrice checks to make sure I haven't eaten to much. And she makes me brush my teeth before I even finish swalowing my food. Aunt Colette never takes me to the movies even tho she says I'm to serious for my age. She says I have a way of always showing up at the rong time. Shes the one I disturbe the most. And with Aunt Diane, I always have to look beutifull, neet and well-dressed. She can't stand seeing a singal spot on my close, a whole in my socks or a hair out of place.

Aunt Elisabeth is as growchy as a bare. She would like me to be a great scolar, at my age. She makes me repete and artickulate every word I say rong. She is in charge of my studys and my future. Then theirs Aunt Florence who wants me to stand on my head with my legs strait up in the air. She does yogga and she thinks I eat to much meat, and not enuff grains and that I'm lacking in spirichuality.

Meanwile, Aunt Gertrude sends me to the corner store at least twenty time a day, to get her a package of pills, a fashun magazine or some new beuty cream. She makes me miss my favorit television shows. So you see, its no fun, the life of an orfan whose not lucky enuff to live in an orfanage. And on top of it all, I don't even have a reel father, a reel mother, a reel brother or sister I can talk too. And I, Rosalie Dansereau, <u>never will</u>.

— *Rosalie Dansereau*

I underlined the title "THE ORFAN" and the last two words, "never will." I wrote the date and I signed my name. I was proud of myself. I had a subject, an outline, and, at last, I had a chance to tell the whole class what it was like to be an orphan.

The next day I wasn't at all nervous. First of all, I had learned my entire presentation by heart. The students listened quietly and then, at the end, they applauded for a long time. Miss LaFrance gave me the best mark I've ever had in my whole life. At the top on my composition, in red, she wrote: "Excellent! Bravo, Rosalie!" And she gave me a big B+.

At the end of the day, lots of friends came to console me. Even Marco, the most annoying wise guy in the class, told me, "You know, Rosalie, I understand you. Your life, well … it's just like mine."

Then he ran off.

I never would have guessed that Marco Tifo was an orphan too! I was so happy, because I'm sure that orphans really understand each other.

• • • •

With my nose glued to my bedroom window, I waited, for what felt like hours, for Aunt Elisabeth to come home. I could hardly wait to show her my big B+ and my "Excellent! Bravo, Rosalie!"

I finally recognized her black briefcase. She was coming up the street. I waited till she went into her room. My heart was beating really fast. With my composition in my hand, I knocked on the door. Inside, I heard her murmur, "Well, well, my cockatoo is early! Is there something wrong? Come in, Rosalie."

As usual, before entering Aunt Elisabeth's room, I took a deep breath. She has so many books in her room, sometimes I think the floor is going to collapse. Since she is very smart and studious, she wears big glasses that make her look like a wise old owl. She really impresses me. Aunt Elisabeth studies the behaviour of monkeys in a laboratory at the university. She says it's absolutely fascinating. I believe her, but that doesn't prevent me from feeling a bit intimidated.

I rushed into her room and told her, "Aunt Elisabeth! Aunt Elisabeth! I think I'm starting to be as smart as you! Look!"

I handed her my composition so she could see the big B+ and the "Excellent! Bravo, Rosalie!" written in red in the upper left-hand corner.

Aunt Elisabeth was beaming like an angel, as she took her glasses off to read. And while she was reading, silently, I suddenly realized …

I realized what a bad subject I had chosen.

A real holy hopping horror of a bad subject.

At first, Aunt Elisabeth just raised her eyebrows and started to frown. Then her eyes seemed to grow bigger and the colour of her face seemed to change.

So I said, "Aunt Elisabeth, I know I shouldn't have … I shouldn't have chosen a subject like that. I should have talked about … about my favourite books or my stamp collection. About the joys of autumn or the terrible agony of a mouse caught in a trap! I realize, Aunt Elisabeth, that I shouldn't have talked about my real father and my real mother, but … I …"

Then, I didn't say another thing.

I was expecting a long sermon on the generous, uncalculating, exemplary love of my seven aunts. And on the infinite lack of gratitude of their little girl, Rosalie.

I wished I could disappear under the piles of books. But there I was, caught in a trap, in a maze with no exit.

Aunt Elisabeth read to the very end. Then she put her owl glasses back on her nose. She looked at me and said, "Do you realize, my dear Rosalie, that I counted exactly fifty-four spelling mistakes in your composition?"

"Are you sure there are *only* fifty-four spelling mistakes in my composition?" I answered without thinking.

"Absolutely sure, my cockatoo. And you must realize that's a lot of mistakes. Too many mistakes for a fourth-grade student."

"Your subject is very good," she went on. "Your outline is perfectly coherent. And heaven knows, there's no lack of imagination in your composition. On the contrary, it's full of good ideas. I understand why you got your B+ and your 'Excellent! Bravo, Rosalie!' But, my cockatoo, you'd better get out your dictionary and your grammar book and correct the fifty-four mistakes if you want anyone to believe you're at all smart. Now off you go! And bring that composition back to me perfectly corrected."

What a holy hopping horror of a holy hopping horror! All week long, I corrected and corrected and corrected. So much so, I ended up neglecting my friend Julie again.

Finally, the following Friday, Aunt Elisabeth told me, "I am very proud of you. Excellent! Bravo, Rosalie! You were able to correct fifty-two of your mistakes. Even though you still have two errors, I never, never would have thought that my cockatoo would be able to correct fifty-two spelling mistakes by the time she was in grade four."

"Me neither, Aunt Elisabeth. I never would have thought so either," I replied.

She came over to me and whispered in my ear, "Tell me, Rosalie, would you like to have a little heart-to-heart talk, just the two of us?"

I had nothing to say. Especially since I knew that Julie was waiting for me on the front steps. So I kissed Aunt Elisabeth on the forehead and, as I walked out the door, I said, "Sure, Aunt Elisabeth, as soon as I get another B+!"

Chapter 3
Peanut

Aunt Diane loves to tell stories. Especially love stories about pale, sad princesses pining away with boredom. Handsome, young princes who are wealthy, courageous and strong always come to their rescue. And Aunt Diane's princesses are always blond with beautiful, blue eyes.

Well, my hair and my eyes are as black as licorice and I'm not remotely sad. Obviously, no handsome, young prince who is wealthy, courageous and strong will ever come to my rescue.

When I dared mention that to Aunt Diane, she answered, "But, Rosalie, my angel, those are just stories. In real life, things are very different!"

"Then tell me a very different story."

That's when Aunt Diane told me the true story of her first love.

Back in those days, boys had a strange way of proving their love to girls. She swears they swallowed all kinds of horrible things, like flies and ants and caterpillars and even spiders.

Her first love's name was Peanut. He was tall and skinny and he had red hair. His cheeks were spattered with freckles. One day, just to prove to Aunt Diane that he wasn't afraid of anything and that he was the bravest boy around, he decided to eat a huge, live horsefly, right before her very eyes. The bug bit him on the tip of his tongue! Poor Peanut yelled and leaped, and took off in a cloud of dust. Aunt Diane never laid eyes on him again.

Marco Tifo doesn't have red hair, but ever since I found out that he was an orphan like me, I've started to look at him in a different way. I wouldn't mind seeing him swallow a few little horrors. But these days, boys have no imagination or courage when they want to prove their love. Most of the time, they just push us around or call us dumb names.

So I decided to find some pretext for getting Marco's attention. We were playing dodge ball in the schoolyard when I got the perfect idea. It came to me in a flash, bright as a 100-watt light bulb, clear as a laser beam.

When I caught Julie's pass, I held onto the ball then threw it with all my might, aiming right at the back of Marco's head. Then I yelled to everyone, "Don't worry, I'll take care of him."

Lying on the ground, half-unconscious, Marco wasn't moving. This was my chance. I knelt down beside him.

"Are you in terrible pain?" I asked.

I lifted his head ever so gently. He opened his eyes and said, "Oww! I think it's broken."

"Do you really think your skull is cracked, poor Marco?"

"Not my skull, Rosalie Dansereau, my foot!" And he tried to stand up.

He was limping, so I took advantage of the situation and let him lean on me. I asked him if he wanted me to walk him home to his orphanage.

"What orphanage?"

"The one where all the orphans live, for holy horror's sake. You're the one who told me the other day that you understood how it felt to be an orphan because your life was just like mine!"

Still leaning on my shoulder, he made a face and said, "Girls never understand a thing. But you can walk me home anyway."

He lives on Garnier Street and it was there, in his father's garage, that he explained everything to me. First he explained that he lives alone with his father and his dog Popsi. And that his real mother didn't die in an airplane accident, like mine. She lives on the other side of the country. He only sees her once a year, during summer vacation. And over the past six years, he's had at least seven different mothers, just like me. It's reached the point where he doesn't count them any more. He told me that the worst one is always his father's latest girlfriend and that, as a matter of fact, the most recent one had been around for the past month. To make matters worse, the latest friend had the awful habit of calling him "sweetie." Marco said he wonders whether his father is his real father, because he hardly ever spends any time alone with him.

"But … are your parents separated?" I asked him, horrified.

"Separated and divorced," he replied.

After he said this, his broken foot suddenly got better. Marco climbed onto a beam in the garage and untied a trapeze and some rings. And right there and then, in spite of his injuries, he showed me at least a dozen dangerous acrobatic tricks. I left promising to go back the next day to see him do his "deadly double-backflip."

• • • •

That evening, while I was polishing Aunt Diane's nails, I swore her to secrecy and told her all about Marco's life. Aunt Diane smiled, and there in her lavender room, she whispered in my ear, "Rosalie, angel, promise me you won't ask him to swallow any creepy, crawly things."

"You mean, like ants and flies and cater-pillars, or other horrible, creepy things like that? Never, Aunt Diane, never, ever. Don't worry, it would never occur to me!"

And I went on polishing Aunt Diane's nails. But secretly my heart was bursting and my head was spinning with a million ideas.

Chapter 4
Hallowe'en

The days were getting shorter. It was dark by four o'clock. In all the store windows on Papineau Street, there were huge pumpkins making faces at the people passing by, and witches with crooked noses, flying around on their broomsticks.

There was even a skeleton dancing a gig on a stack of canned goods at our own corner store. That's where Aunt Gertrude and I bought our two big pumpkins. One for Aunt Alice's pies and the other one to put in the window that looks out onto the boulevard.

The night before Hallowe'en, we all got together to carve the pumpkin. We pulled out the orange mane where dozens of seeds were hidden. Aunt Beatrice roasted them in the oven. Aunt Gertrude saved a handful for the sparrows.

As usual, I was in charge of carving the jack'o'lantern. With a felt pen, I outlined sneaky eyes. I drew a pointed nose and a mouth with scary teeth. Aunt Diane cut out the face with a sharp knife. Then we put a candle inside and turned out all the lights.

Phew! I'd done it again! My pumpkin was a real success. One holy hopping horror of a mean-looking monster! Sitting there in the window the next day, it would attract all the vampires, gnomes, evil spirits and skeletons in the neighbourhood. I was sure of it!

Aunt Gertrude turned the lights back on and asked me, "Well, monster, what do you think we should dress up as this year?"

"This year, ummm, this year," I stuttered, "I'm ... I'm going out trick-or-treating alone! I mean, alone with my friends. Everything is all organized! We're going to put our costumes on at Julie's house. Marise Cormier, her brother Simon and Marco Tifo will be there too. I promise I'll be home by nine thirty."

My aunts just stared at me with their mouths hanging open, like seven goldfish in a bowl.

"I swear, cross my heart, for holy hopping horror's sake."

"Don't swear and don't say those awful words," Sergeant Celery replied.

"I assume there'll be an adult with you?" Aunt Gertrude asked.

"Holy horrors, we're not babies any more! All my friends have permission to go out alone."

Then, in a very strange tone of voice, Aunt Gertrude said, "Monster, the problem is that at your age, you're not aware of certain dangers. Aside from the automobile accidents, sometimes there are ... individuals who aren't quite normal who take advantage of a night like that to ... to harm children ..."

"You mean those weird maniacs who offer us candy and invite us into their cars? Or into some back room of their house? Holy horrors, Aunt Gertrude, you don't have to worry about that. We had a two-hour session on all that at school. The principal explained everything to us."

"I'm sure she did, chickadee," said my Aunt Alice, quite distressed. "But we'll simply be too worried if one of us doesn't go along with you."

I could see the seven of them, already in the depths of despair, and I found them perfectly ridiculous. I thought about it briefly and then, totally exasperated, I said, "If I can't go out alone with my friends, I won't go out at all! I'd be too ashamed to be the only one my age with her parents. I got rid of my diapers and my bottle years ago and — holy hopping — I'm ... I'm not a baby anymore!"

I went racing upstairs and slammed the door to my room, sure I'd hear seven voices yell in unison:

"Don't slam your door, Rosalie!"

• • • •

The next morning, for the first time in my life, I got permission to go trick-or-treating without having one of my aunts spy on me. I was pretty proud of myself. I had the strange feeling that I had aged twelve years in one fell swoop.

Julie's mother lent us her entire make-up

case, all her out-of-style dresses, her old curtains and cast-off wigs. In one box I even found an old, yellow bedspread.

An hour later, Marise was a beautiful princess from the Middle Ages, her brother Simon was a Star Wars robot, Julie was an atomic ant, Marco was a one-eyed pirate, and I ... I was the Abominable Snowwoman!

• • • •

The street was teeming with monsters, animals, robots, toads, princesses and countesses. In almost every window, glowing pumpkins beckoned to the costumed children. We were pushing and shoving on the stairs, sticking out our loot bags to collect handfuls of caramels, apples, taffy candies, pennies and dimes.

Marise, Simon, Julie and I had reached the dark side streets in our neighbourhood. Our bags were getting heavier from door to door. Simon already found his too heavy to carry. He started whining and dragging behind. He didn't want to climb up any more stairs, but he didn't want to stay alone at the foot of the stairs either. Marise was so mad,

she swore she'd never bring her little brother along again because he was such a baby.

Suddenly, Simon stopped complaining. He pointed toward a white shape hiding between two cars.

"It's only a ghost, Simon Cormier!" Marco Tifo told him. "Walk ahead of us if you're such a scaredy-cat!"

"Don't you think," Julie asked, "that that ghost is a bit big?"

"Ghosts are always big," replied Simon, trying to reassure himself.

"What do you know about ghosts, Simon Cormier? I agree with Julie. I think he's too big," Marise concluded.

Without admitting it to each other, all five of us were convinced we were dealing with one of those terrible child molesters.

Marco suggested we change streets. Marise was in such a hurry, she tripped on her princess's dress. She fell flat on the sidewalk and the contents of her trick-or-treat bag spilled out onto the street. Apples, pears, dimes and pennies went rolling all over the place.

"The ghost is following us!" Simon screamed. "The ghost is following us!"

We took off like a flock of frightened pigeons, leaving Marise's bag behind. We went running into my aunts' house screaming, "A maniac! A maniac!"

Julie explained how big he was. Marise told how ugly he was. Simon had seen, with his very own eyes, a long knife. Marco described how the ghost wove in and out of the parked cars as he chased us down the street.

And as for me, I confirmed that it was one holy hopping horror of a true story.

Marise felt miserable just thinking about her trick-or-treat bag lying on the sidewalk in Fabre Street. Just as Marco, playing hero, offered to go and bring back whatever he could — whoosh! — the door flew open!

The ghost came leaping into the room! It was squirming around like a vampire at high noon. All tangled up in its white sheet, in a very upset voice, it yelled, "They all got away from me! They got away from me!"

Then, from under the white sheet, Aunt Gertrude's head appeared!

Surprised and disappointed, all of us said, "What? Don't tell me you're our maniac!"

Really embarrassed, Aunt Gertrude stuttered, "Well ... well, I still like to get dressed up too! I like going trick-or-treating! Just because I seem like an old lady doesn't mean I don't still enjoy having a good time!"

Aunt Alice explained to Aunt Gertrude how Marise had been so frightened by the huge ghost that she'd lost her trick-or-treat bag.

Aunt Gertrude flashed a most mysterious smile.

"Don't move," she said. "Don't budge an inch! I'll be right back!"

She went out onto the porch and came back carrying a pillowcase bursting at the seams. Her Hallowe'en ghost's bag was overflowing with candy! She passed it to Marise and said, "For the most beautiful princess from the Middle Ages, courtesy of the oldest Hallowe'en ghost in town!"

Marise emptied out her enormous sack while the rest of us went through our little bags. Then we had some pumpkin pie and chatted about ghosts and maniacs. But something was bothering me. In fact, I still can't figure it out.

Just how had Aunt Gertrude managed to spy on us and still come home with such a huge haul?

With my mouth full of candy, I warned everyone, "I just want you all to know that next year I'm dressing up as a holy hopping horrible ghost!"

Chapter 5
The Angel

When I got up this morning, everything had changed. The sky, the trees, the street, the telephone wires and even the sparrows perched on the wires — everything, absolutely everything, was white.

Snow, soft and white as cotton batting, was falling. Winter was here, at last! And Christmas was finally on its way!

In my house, winter also means an endless series of:

"Cover your neck, loveheart, you'll catch cold!"

"Tie your scarf, angel, and don't forget to take your vitamin C!"

"Blow your nose, monster, and change your socks. They're soaking wet!"

"Don't tell me my ladybug has lost her mittens again! Blow your nose again, ladybug."

"Could you shake the snow off your clothes before you come in, chickadee?"

"Sweetness, are you sure your feet are warm enough? There's no surer way to catch a cold. Why don't you blow your nose?"

"My cockatoo's cheeks are frozen! Wipe your boots on the doormat. Oh, no, you've lost your mittens again! Why don't you blow your nose?"

And that's the way it is from the very first snowfall on.

● ● ● ●

Last week I had some good news for Aunt Colette, who wants to become the greatest actress of modern times.

In order to get to her behind her Chinese screen, I had to climb over a pile of clothes, mountains of movie magazines, dozens of pairs of worn-out shoes, a transistor radio, an alto flute, a soprano flute, a violin case and an African tam-tam.

Curled up on her plush-covered divan, Aunt Colette was dreaming.

She started when I put my hands over her eyes and said, "Guess what?"

"Oh! You scared me, sweetness," she said with an amused twinkle in her eye. "Give me a little hint. What do I have to guess?"

"Well, it's something that's going to make you holy horribly, enormously, incredibly, terrifically happy!"

"You got two free tickets to the movies?"

"You're not even warm! I think I'm going to have to tell you, because you'll never guess! You know that every Christmas the school organizes a big pageant. Well, for the first time in my life, I, Rosalie, got a part!"

Aunt Colette jumped up. She did three pirouettes, hugged me and kissed me at least ten times all over my cheeks.

I finally managed to say, "And in this year's pageant, I'm going to be an angel."

"An angel? An angel? Why, that's ridiculous, sweetness!"

"It's not ridiculous at all, because we're telling the story of the arrival of the Three Wise Men at the manger in Bethlehem!"

"The arrival of the Three Wise Men at the manger in Bethlehem?" she repeated, obviously dismayed. "I thought you were taking the Moral Education course, sweetness!"

"I was, at first," I replied, "but I changed. I like the Catechism course better. We read lots of stories. Like the one where little David kills mean Goliath with his slingshot. And the one where the seven jealous brothers push their youngest brother Joseph into the well."

"And I suppose," asked Aunt Colette, "that you also go to mass?"

"Sometimes. I go to talk to the angel."

"What? What angel, sweetness?" Aunt Colette asked me, flabbergasted.

"The plaster angel, for holy horror's sake! He's so old, part of his nose is missing, but he has such a nice smile. He says 'yes' whenever we slip a coin into his little basket."

"It sounds like this angel never says 'no.'"

Aunt Colette seemed lost in her thoughts for a minute, then she said, "Tell me a bit more about your part in the big school pageant."

I explained that my part wasn't at all difficult. After the Wise Men offer the gold,

53

frankincense and the myrrh to Mary, I, hanging from a wire, am supposed to trumpet:

"Hosanna on the highest!"

And then, "Unto us a child is born!"

Over the next few days, Aunt Colette helped me rehearse my two lines.

And on the evening of the big day, my seven aunts arrived at the school wearing their party dresses.

• • • •

There I was in the wings, with my two pink wings firmly strapped to my back and an acrobat's belt carefully wrapped around my waist, anxiously waiting for the curtain to rise.

After the final chords of a Mozart duet performed by two grade six students, the curtain finally rose.

I saw my seven aunts sitting in the center of the first row. With a tiny wave of her hand, Aunt Colette let me know that she had seen me, too.

The cow twitched her wool tail and the donkey brayed loudly. Joseph stood there leaning on his cane, watching Mary rock the Baby Jesus.

One by one, the Wise Men presented their gifts. I sat on my cardboard rock nervously waiting for the rope to lift me into the air. Two other students from my class, who were playing the second and third angels, were also waiting.

I finally felt a little tug at my waist and, slowly, my body rose above the manger. I took a deep breath, stared into the darkness at the back of the hall and proclaimed:

"HOSANNA ..."

Then the voices of my seven prompters chimed in loudly, "...on the highest!"

I was so startled, I stuttered the next line almost inaudibly: "Unto ... unto ... us ... a child is ... is born."

The worst was yet to come. My seven aunts all stood up and applauded wildly. It sounded like a horrendous thunderstorm.

Hanging there in the air, in front of hundreds of people, I saw the lights flicker. I blinked my eyes, then closed them.

"Holy hopping horror of a holy hopping horror of a holy hopping horror!" I repeated over and over.

In the racket of my aunts' applause, no

one could hear the second and third angels screaming their lungs out:

"Let us praise him!"

"Let us adore him!"

Not only did I almost die of embarrassment that evening, but my aunts made a couple of enemies for life: the mothers of the second and third angels.

When I got home, my wings were slightly crushed and my heart was heavy. To console me, Aunt Colette said, "Don't worry, sweetness, you were the prettiest angel. And no one ever would have guessed you were embarrassed. You have a memory like an elephant and you're as graceful as a swallow. You have everything you need to become the greatest actress of modern times. And most of all, sweetness, did you hear the thunderous applause?!"

Most of all, I'd realized that evening how much my seven aunts had a knack for making my life miserable.

Humiliated, I ran up the stairs and slammed the door to my room. And not one of my aunts dared yell:

"Don't slam your door, Rosalie!"

That evening they held their second official

family council. And, undoubtedly to win my forgiveness, they decided to make me really happy.

On Christmas eve, for the first time ever, all seven of my aunts attended Midnight Mass with me.

I was so happy to finally be able to show them the old angel who nodded his head and had a broken nose.

After mass, among the gilded columns and the Christmas trees with their ornaments and lights, as the organ played and the choir sang, my seven aunts and I went over to the statue.

I looked the angel in the eye and murmured softly, "Beautiful angel who smiles at me so sweetly, could you spread your wings and fly into the sky? Could you find my real mother and tell her how much I miss her? And for holy hopping horror's sake, if you do find her, will you please let me know?"

And I slipped the seven dimes my aunts had given me into his basket. The angel nodded his head, seven times, and answered, "YES, YES, YES, YES, YES, YES, YES."

Chapter 6
Popsi!

To this day, Marco Tifo has never swallowed the tiniest holy hopping horror for me. But on three different occasions he has almost broken his neck trying to show me his "deadly double-backflip."

One afternoon last week, I found him huddled in the back of his garage. He was in no mood for deadly backflips and even seemed to be sniffling.

With springtime taking so long to come, and the damp winds that still smelled of the North Pole, I thought maybe Marco had caught the flu.

"Do you have a temperature?" I asked him.

"That's not what's wrong!"

"So, you're sulking!"

"I'm not sulking, Rosalie Dansereau, I'm sad, that's all."

"Why are you whining like a baby, Marco Tifo?" I said unsympathetically.

That's when he told me how his dog Popsi got run over by a car in the wee small hours of the morning.

Marco was so sad, so desperate that even I, Rosalie Dansereau, couldn't think of anything to say to comfort him. I sat down beside him in the back of the garage and we cried together.

When I got home, my eyes were all swollen. Sergeant Celery noticed it right away.

"Has my loveheart been crying? Tell me which one of your friends has upset you like this!"

"It's because Marco's dog died," I yelled. "And no one, at least no big person, can possibly understand."

And I started to cry again.

"Don't cry, chickadee," said Aunt Alice, stroking my hair.

"Go ahead and cry, ladybug, it'll make

you feel better," Aunt Florence chimed in, as she patted me on the shoulder.

"It was just a dog, and he was really old," said Aunt Beatrice.

"He wasn't just a dog and he wasn't that old. He was only eight, and he was Popsi, Marco's only dog!"

"It wasn't your dog, ladybug, and you hardly knew him," added Aunt Florence as she tried to lead me to her room so we could have a quiet talk.

"No, I don't feel like it! I don't feel like it!" I yelled at Aunt Florence, pulling away from her. "I don't want to go to your room and talk about it! I don't want to meditate or stand on my head with my legs straight up in the air! I can't do a headstand and I'll never be able to do a headstand! I don't want you to tell me that death is life and life is death. And that suffering brings maturity and spirituality! Because I, Rosalie Dansereau, don't know what that means! I don't want to hear about how happy my father and mother are in their heaven. And that Marco's dog has gone to join them there! I just want ... I just want Marco to stop feeling sad. Because even if his dog was just a dog, even if he was old, even if he was homely as a dirty mop and he barked all the time, he was Marco's dog! And it's seeing Marco so sad that's making me cry."

Aunt Florence shrugged her shoulders and two big tears rolled down her cheeks. She headed toward the stairs.

I didn't know what to do. I followed her into her room. Aunt Florence was curled up on her bed, sobbing. I wished I could have erased everything I'd just said. I just stood there, not knowing how to console her.

I knew that Aunt Florence was always crying at the drop of a hat. And that her latest boyfriend had just left her.

Suddenly, I felt the way I had felt with Marco in the back of his garage. So I just sat down beside her and cried along with her for a long time.

Then, I put a pillow on the floor, placed my head on it, and I lifted my legs.

For the very first time in my life, I succeeded. Aunt Florence raised her head.

I lost my balance the minute she looked at me. Then, both of us cried some more.

Chapter 7
Miss Brochette

Spring at last! All the troubles of winter have melted away with the snow.

As far as I'm concerned, it's simple, there are three things I love most in the whole world: shepherd's pie, pistachio ice cream and springtime, so I can go rollerskating.

As soon as the snow disappeared, I got out my skates. I met Marise Cormier and Julie Savard and we went rolling down the sidewalk, speeding along like comets, so fast that Marco and Simon had trouble keeping up with us on their bicycles.

Marise and Julie both had brand-new rollerskates, but I still had my same old skates from last year. My aunts have the terrible habit of buying things a size too big.

"You'll grow into them, Rosalie, you'll grow into them, Rosalie," they always sigh, as if growing up were some inevitable tragedy.

For me, the real tragedy was that my aunts had decided that my old rollerskates could see me through another season. Personally, I didn't agree. And it was right around the corner on Papineau Street, standing in front of the biggest window of the biggest store, that I became absolutely convinced they were wrong.

There they were, dazzlingly white with dozens of little stars made out of silver and gold sequins sewn right into the leather. On top of one of the skates, written on a piece of cardboard, a sign read:

SUPER SPECIAL: $29.95

Believe me, these rollerskates were completely different from my two old horrors of skates that had turned yellow and had brakes that only worked when they felt like it, maybe half the time.

Marise, Julie and even Simon and Marco all agreed with me. Since Julie can count as fast as a calculator, I asked her, "$29.95

divided by seven, exactly how much does that make?"

"$4.27 and … six sevenths," she replied.

"Holy cow! $4.27 and six sevenths, that's peanuts."

As I headed home, I could see myself going to see each of my aunts in her respective room. I'd explain the situation to them, one by one. Just thinking about it seemed to give me wings.

I was skating so fast I could barely hear Julie and Marise yelling, way behind me, "Wait for us, Rosalie! Wait for us!"

Then, at the corner of Papineau and St. Joseph Boulevard, everything went wrong. I tried to brake: Crash, scrunch, plop! It was too late!

My head had already gone barrelling into a soft belly. Crushed on the sidewalk under one of my skates, there was a hat — a hat I recognized all too well. It belonged to Miss Brochette — better known by the neighborhood kids as "The Witch of St. Joseph Boulevard."

By some weird stroke of fate, it was the second time that week my head had gone barrelling into her soft belly. Just like the first time, she let out a desperate shriek as she put her hat back on her head. And once again, totally furious, she dragged me home to my aunts.

In spite of all my apologies, I found myself back on our front porch with the old hag standing there beside me, leaning on the door-bell.

At first, my seven horrified aunts politely listened to her screech. Miss Brochette made it clear to them that I was a real bird-brain. That I was as sneaky as a weasel, as sly as a skunk, as dangerous as a snake. And that I rolled down the sidewalk like a bulldog. That I was a public menace, a disaster for humanity — and, most of all, a disaster for hats.

To prove her point, she showed them her awful old hat. Aunt Diane and Aunt Gertrude burst out laughing in spite of themselves.

I tried to tell the witch that it wasn't me who had squished her hat. It was the brakes on my holy hopping horrible old rollerskates that had refused to work.

Insulted, Miss Brochette shook her finger at me and hissed, "Mark my words, next time

I'm going to complain to the authorities!"

As she stomped off, she turned back, glared at me from under her torn veil, and threatened, "Does the word POLICE mean anything to you, young lady?"

The door closed. Aunt Beatrice turned to me and said, "Rosalie, dear, there'll be no more rollerskating for the next three days. Do you hear me?"

Neither Aunt Alice, nor Aunt Colette, nor Aunt Diane, nor Aunt Elisabeth, nor Aunt Florence, nor Aunt Gertrude said another word.

• • • •

Three days is a long time to be deprived of one of the three things you love most in the whole world. But three days go by all too quickly when you're trying to raise $4.27 and six sevenths times seven.

In other words, $29.95 to buy the most wonderful pair of star-spangled skates I'd ever seen. The kind of rollerskates that brake at the sight of any old witch on any old boulevard.

Since my friends always have great ideas, I invited them all over to my house. I was sure none of my aunts could hear us. We sat on the floor of my room and thought hard.

At first we came up with lots of dangerous ideas, like robbing a bank. Marco even suggested the local Credit Union where he had seen piles, bags, mountains of money. Julie thought it would be better for me to count how much I had in my own bank. I emptied out my piggybank. There was exactly eighty-eight cents. I explained that with my seven aunts, it was always someone's birthday. And that I had emptied my bank for Aunt Alice's present just last month.

Then Marise got her tooth idea. The tooth that's loose and finally falls out and you put it under your pillow. The next morning you wake up and find a small fortune in its place. Marise tried to wiggle all twenty-eight of my teeth, but not a single one was the least bit loose. Simon very generously offered me his last tiny baby tooth. It was just hanging by a thread, but no one had the courage to pull it out.

Finally, there were serious, boring solutions, like running errands, returning empty bottles, taking babies for walks, or taking out

the garbage. Julie, our calculator, approved of these solutions. But she thought it would be impossible to save $29.07 in three days, especially since we had to go to school from eight thirty in the morning till three thirty in the afternoon.

Julie is always right. We had to find an activity we could organize on Monday, Tuesday and Wednesday, between four o'clock and six o'clock in the afternoon. We needed a brilliant idea to hit the jackpot.

That's when Aunt Alice gently knocked on my door and whispered, "It's me, chickadee. I've brought you and your friends a pitcher of lemonade."

After all that thinking, we were thirsty. We emptied our glasses in one fell swoop and, suddenly, we all had the same idea: A LEMONADE STAND!

Where? At the bus stop on Papineau Street. When all the students and the workers are on their way home! All it would take was a little table and a sign:

SUPER SPECIAL
25¢ a glass

Simon promised to bring a big pitcher of grape lemonade. Marise would bring orange juice, Marco some grenadine, and Julie apple juice. And I'd bring some ice and another pitcher of lemonade — plain lemonade-lemonade.

After a few calculations, Julie was convinced that we could make all the money we needed to buy the famous rollerskates.

I was ecstatic by the time my friends left. I found it really hard to keep my secret and not to tell my aunts everything.

At ten past four on Monday afternoon, we were all set up. Marco had helped me carry the table. I'd made a sign, and the five pitchers of juice were all lined up. Beside them was a stack of little paper cups I'd found in the back of one of the kitchen cupboards.

We were feverishly awaiting the arrival of the first bus and our first customers. Finally, the number 22 Papineau Street bus drew to a stop. An old man with a white beard stepped out. He came over to us and asked what flavour refreshments we had. He had a very fancy accent.

"These aren't refreshments, sir," Simon explained. "It's real lemonade."

"Ah, excellent," said the old man, "so much the better!"

He ordered a glass of Simon's grape lemonade and handed me a dollar.

Taken by surprise, I realized that no one had thought of bringing any change. The old gentleman drank slowly, then he thanked us.

"Your grape lemonade is absolutely delicious!" he said. "You can keep the change. It's so rare these days that people take the time to tend to their customers!"

Then he walked away slowly.

Julie ran to the corner store to get change for the dollar.

Reassured, we waited for the second bus, then the third.

An hour later, Julie reported that we had collected the fabulous sum of $8.50.

Then, suddenly, everything was ruined. A few drops of rain were followed by a real downpour. The passengers getting off the buses ran off in all directions. We were determined to stand by our pitchers of lemonade, but we finally had to give in. Soaking wet, we closed down our stand and agreed to meet, same time, same place, the next day.

• • • •

Instead of meeting on Papineau Street the next day, the five of us found ourselves huddled in my bedroom. It was raining cats and dogs outside. And to top it all off, the TV weather forecast called for the same holy horrible weather the following day.

We had to come up with a new plan. We were still missing $20.57. How could we find that much money in one day when it was raining out?

That's when I had the most extraordinary idea — what if I begged for money?

Once I'd watched a television report on a country a bit different from ours. And I'd seen children begging. Marco said that he had seen the same show. And Simon remembered that the sadder, the more disabled the children were, the more money adults gave them. It was such a good idea, Julie couldn't even begin to calculate how much money we might make.

Marco offered to bring a couple of umbrellas and an old wheelchair that was hanging around in his father's garage. Julie would push the chair and Simon would hold out his hand and say:

73

"Charity, please! For my sister, she's very sick."

Marise would be in charge of the first aid kit. It would have bandages, a bottle of ketchup, a bottle of iodine and a vial of Methylene Blue. She promised that was all she'd need to turn me into the sickest, the saddest, the most pathetic disabled girl imaginable.

My job was to practice staring into space, without seeing a thing. I had the entire evening to get used to it.

At supper that evening, my seven puzzled aunts were convinced that I was coming down with a terrible flu or an unavoidable contagious disease. I looked so miserable, they smothered me with attention and kisses. By the time I fell asleep, I was convinced that the whole world would believe that I was sick, sad and disabled.

• • • •

When we emerged from Marco's father's garage, all five of us were huddled under the two umbrellas. I was sitting hunched over in the wheelchair, and Julie was pushing me along the boulevard towards the Papineau Street bus stop.

With an iodine-soaked bandage on my forehead, my arm in a sling, and my knees stained with ketchup and Methylene Blue, I looked pretty strange. Julie said I looked like I'd just been run over by a ten-ton truck.

Personally, I thought I looked more like Frankenstein just after he'd finished off a huge pot of tomato sauce.

Black and blue all over, and wrapped up like a mummy, I sat there trying to concentrate on the saddest thing in the world: having to put up with my old rollerskates for another whole year!

As we turned the corner, I saw HER hat. Miss Brochette stopped dead in her tracks and watched us go by. At last, she made up her mind and walked over to us.

Holy hopping horrible holy hopping horrors! What a catastrophe! *Please*, don't let Simon ask her for charity, I said to myself.

There was no need. Without recognizing me, she slipped ten cents into my hand and exclaimed, "Poor child! No wonder she can't stand the sun!"

And she went on her way.

Through clenched teeth, I muttered, "Why did she say I can't stand the sun?"

In fact, it was perfectly obvious: the sun was shining brightly and there we were, all five of us, crowded like sardines under our umbrellas.

Julie decided that if, on top of being sick, sad, and disabled, I couldn't stand the sun, that was a fine reason for not closing our umbrellas.

And so it was under our umbrellas at the bus stop that we began our great plea for charity.

At first, it was dimes and quarters that students in a hurry slipped into Simon's hand. Then came the dollar bills. As we collected more and more money, I started to feel embarrassed and closed my eyes.

At quarter to six, Julie announced that we had enough money to buy three pairs of skates.

At that very moment, I opened my eyes and saw Aunt Alice getting off the bus. She came over to Simon, who had his hand stretched out. Like a robot, he kept repeating, "Charity, please! For my little sister who's very sick."

Aunt Alice walked around Simon, touched me on the shoulder and said, "Aren't you ashamed of yourself, chickadee?"

Then she walked away.

"It's all over!" I told my friends. "Back to the garage, quick! Because, because … Holy hopping horrors, I'll explain it all tomorrow!"

Aunt Alice didn't say a thing to my other aunts. I explained everything to her, absolutely everything. My holy horrible skates that didn't brake anymore, Miss Brochette, the star-spangled skates in the store window, the lemonade stand, the rain and the idea of begging.

And Aunt Alice understood everything. She even came with me to see the skates with the gold and silver stars in the biggest window of the biggest store on Papineau Street.

I went with her to have the brakes on my rollerskates repaired. Afterwards, Aunt Alice sewed on beautiful sequin stars. She even sewed a gigantic star, as bright as a comet, on my skating sweater.

As for the money we collected, Aunt Alice told me that someday my friends and I would know who to give it to. Personally, I still don't know. My friends don't either. But I do know one thing. Thanks to Aunt Alice, I have the most beautiful skates in the world. And the next time I meet Miss Brochette's hat at the corner of the street, my brakes are going to work!

Chapter 8
Charcoal

I don't know why on that particular day, the last Sunday in May, I found my room so boring. I still had my collection of teddy bears from Aunt Alice, Aunt Beatrice's Lego blocks, two Cabbage Patch dolls from Aunt Colette, Aunt Diane's china knickknacks, Aunt Elisabeth's rows and rows of books, and Aunt Florence's trucks, cars, robots and airplanes. And my latest present — a radio-cassette-player from Aunt Gertrude.

The seven colour photographs of my seven aunts were all there, displayed on the wall over my bed, and just beneath them was the picture of me as a baby, chewing on my pacifier.

I didn't know what to do with myself. I picked up a book called *The Gilded Cage*. I finally gave up trying to read it and decided to go out and roam up and down St. Joseph Boulevard.

The air smelled sweet. The lilacs were exploding in Mrs. Dumas's yard, the third house over. Their purple blossoms were so heavy they almost touched the grass. I couldn't resist and went over to breathe in their perfume. Mrs. Dumas was sitting on her front porch.

"You can cut yourself a bouquet, if you want, Rosalie," she called to me.

Just as I was about to answer, her big grey cat leapt onto the porch. And four little kittens came bouncing along right behind her.

I forgot all about the lilacs and ran over to the cats. I grabbed the smallest one, the one that was as black as charcoal. His fur felt as soft as a chick's downy feathers.

"Do you think I could have one like this?" I asked Mrs. Dumas. "I'd make a little bed for him in my room. I'd feed him and he'd grow big and fat. He'd be my very own cat."

"I certainly can't keep them all," Mrs. Dumas replied. "They're weaned now. And since I'm not Mother Goose, I'd be happy to give you one — but you'd better ask your aunts first!"

I looked closely at the black kitten, then set him down beside the others. I decided immediately that I'd call him Charcoal. And off I ran, promising Mrs. Dumas that I'd be back to pick him up the next day.

That evening at supper — I'll never forget it — we were having fish and everyone was in a good mood. It had been a long time since the eight of us had had a meal together. My aunts were in such a jolly mood, it seemed like the perfect time to broach the subject.

"Mrs. Dumas's cat had four kittens and the littlest one, who's as black as charcoal, really likes me."

I looked around the table. Suddenly my seven aunts seemed very busy eating. They stared into their plates. I screwed up my nerve and tried again.

"Mrs. Dumas wants to find homes for some of them and … I think she wants to give the little one to me."

Seven forks froze in mid-air. Discouraged, in a little squeak of a voice, I added, "For holy hopping horrors' sake, I'd really like to take care of it — upstairs, in my room."

Silence reigned all around the table. Even Aunt Beatrice, who usually swallows everything whole, began chewing very, very slowly. Aunt Alice was the first one to speak.

"Don't you realize, chickadee, that a black cat would bring bad luck?"

Aunt Beatrice finally swallowed her mouthful, wrinkled her nose and said, "Cats have all sorts of germs! Furthermore, the whole house would smell awful. You'd better forget that idea, Rosalie."

Then Aunt Colette said, "I'm allergic to cats. Just looking at them makes my eyes puffy."

Aunt Diane ran her hand down my back and sighed, "There would be fur everywhere.

And who would take care of him during the day?"

As for Aunt Elisabeth, she preferred monkeys, or, in a pinch, she could put up with a dog.

Aunt Florence suggested a canary. Then, Aunt Gertrude concluded, "You know very well, monster, that cats scare away the birds. They eat sparrows, and the swallows and the finches will never, ever come near the house again!"

Fortunately, that evening Aunt Alice had poached a boneless fish and no one choked to death. The cream sauce in my plate had hardened. And I couldn't stop the tears from running down my cheeks.

Between two sobs, I managed to say, "Every one of you keeps whatever she chooses in her room. Aunt Alice, you have all your cookbooks and even your pillows smell of flour, vanilla and molasses. Aunt Beatrice, I know what you have hidden in your dresser drawer! A picture of Alphonse, your boyfriend who lives in Abitibi! And Aunt Colette has all those giant posters in her room because she dreams of becoming a great movie star. I know that

Aunt Diane is going to get married soon. Aunt Elisabeth's room is going to collapse under the weight of her books. Aunt Florence's room always smells of incense. Aunt Gertrude's room is full of bottles of make-up and beauty cream, and magazines and newspapers. And in my room, all there is … is everything you've chosen for me … everything you've given me! But now I'd like to be able to choose something for myself! I …"

I needed to wipe my nose so badly, I ran up to my room. I curled up in a ball on my bed. It felt like the whole world was unfair and that I was the only child on earth who didn't have "someone" or "something" to take care of and love.

I lay there in the dark and imagined the worst tortures possible for each of my aunts.

Alice was burning in hell, eternally.

Beatrice was plowing a celery field in Abitibi.

Colette was allergic to the air and covered with a rash. She scratched herself day and night with no relief.

Diane was tangled up in a cocoon of fur, and nobody, not even Peanut, her old swallower of horrors, came to set her free.

Elisabeth, imprisoned in a giant maze, was looking for a way out. Two monkeys dressed in white lab coats were observing her progress.

Florence had turned so yellow, she had been planted by mistake in a garden of daffodils. And she had to keep repeating: "I am not a canary! I am not a canary!"

Gertrude, who as far as I was concerned deserved the worst punishment, had to swallow whole, in front of my cat, Charcoal, one of every species of bird found in Canada.

And then, holy hopping horrors, I felt a little better. I finally fell asleep. Little did I realize that I had brought about the third and longest official family council.

● ● ● ●

The following morning I left for school without saying a word to my aunts. And I came home sulking. In spite of my seven aunts' repeated efforts to cheer me up, I ate supper gritting my teeth.

Around eight o'clock, I went up to my room. And sure that my real mother, up there in her heaven, understood me, I curled up in my bed.

At exactly nine o'clock, Aunt Beatrice came in as usual. She put the obligatory glass of water on my dresser, pushed my teddybear around, tucked in my quilt and looked like she was headed for the door. Then she turned around and slipped a necklace into my hand. And disappeared!

When I turned on my light, I saw that I was holding a golden chain with a little china heart. And on the heart was a drawing of a little black cat.

I don't even dare say what crossed my mind. Then the door opened again. Aunt Colette put a straw basket down on my quilt. She stayed long enough to say, "It's for your doll, sweetness. Sleep tight! I can't stay, I'm in a hurry!"

Then came:

Aunt Diane with a ball of yarn,

Aunt Elisabeth with a brand new brush,

Aunt Florence with a pile of old newspapers.

When Aunt Gertrude finally slipped into my room with a bowl of fresh milk, I, Rosalie Dansereau, had figured everything out.

I knew that when Aunt Alice brought me her two molasses cookies, tucked inside her sweater I would find Charcoal, my little black kitten.

• • • •

Looking at Charcoal sleeping in his straw basket that night, I was sure that I was at least seven times luckier, seven times more loved, than anyone else in the whole world.

Epilogue

A whole year has gone by since Charcoal arrived in my life. There haven't been any other official family councils. And things haven't changed much around our house.

Aunt Alice, my gentle aunt, still slips two molasses cookies under my pillow every night.

Aunt Beatrice, Sergeant Celery, is still supervising, and will always supervise, everything.

Aunt Colette is advertising toothpaste on television. Evenings, she's acting in a silly play. She's playing the part of an angel. "It's experimental," she says, "and not the least bit ridiculous!"

Aunt Diane is in the middle of a great love story with a prince who teaches geography in a high school nearby.

Aunt Elisabeth is still observing her monkeys' progress in her huge laboratory at the university. She says they are often more interesting than human beings, but she still insists upon correcting my homework.

Aunt Florence cries as often as ever. Fortunately, she has given up all hope of getting me to stand on my head with my legs straight up in the air. She says I have no talent for it whatsoever.

And last but not least, Aunt Gertrude is managing a beauty salon. She still refuses to reveal the secret of her fabulous success as a ghost on our famous Hallowe'en outing.

Marise and Simon are still my friends. Julie, on the other hand, spends much too much time with her new computer. She finds it "super fun!"

Marco Tifo still hasn't forgotten his dog Popsi. He consoles himself with his new electric guitar. Yesterday, he almost succeeded in doing his deadly double-backflip. But I'm always afraid he'll crack his skull.

And Charcoal, my cat, has gotten so big and fat I've had to put him on a diet. I suspect my aunts feed him when I'm not looking. He's not always well-behaved. Sometimes he manages to make some holy hopping horrible messes. But I can't really get too mad at him! After all, he's still such an itty-bitty baby cat.

I almost forgot! A new boy moved into the third floor of the house next door. His name is Pierre-Yves and his nose is covered with freckles. He's not an orphan at all. He has a little white female cat who's always running around everywhere.

I thought I should warn Charcoal. I trapped him between my pillow and my old teddybear, looked him in the eye and said, "You're much too young to go gallivanting with that pretty cat next door, do you hear me?"

He just purred as usual, and scampered off like one holy hopping horribly, badly brought-up cat!

THE ROSALIE SERIES CONTINUES IN 1995!

Rosalie's Battles

R osalie is back! And so are her seven mothers, her two cats and her gang of friends. This time, Rosalie's adventure begins when a schoolyard snowball fight turns sour and becomes "war." While Rosalie learns some truths about real war from the Vietnamese immigrant Piam Low, her new kitten goes missing and her friend Pierre-Yves is hospitalized with pneumonia. Will Rosalie's battles never end? Find out how Rosalie's busy life unfolds, in this second irresistible book in the series.

ISBN 0-921556-50-0
$ 5.95 paperback (not available in the US)

ISBN 0-921556-51-9
$10.95 hardcover

The Rosalie Series
by Ginette Anfousse
Illustrated by Marisol Sarrazin
Translated by Linda Gaboriau

Rosalie has returned, and this time she has a big dream: to be the best tapdancer in North America. But trouble begins when Rosalie reveals her ambition to her best friend, Julie Morin. Julie, who is always right and knows everything, is not impressed. Nor are Rosalie's seven mothers, and nor is her friend Pierre-Yves. Can Rosalie become a young Fred Astaire, despite her lack of natural ability? In her third thrilling adventure, Rosalie gets herself in and out of trouble and along the way discovers a few things about the nature of friendship and the value of dreams.

ISBN 0-921556-52-7
$ 5.95 paperback (not available in the US)

ISBN 0-921556-53-5
$10.95 hardcover

MORE BOOKS BY RAGWEED PRESS

Next Teller: A Book of Canadian Storytelling
Collected by Dan Yashinsky

Thirty-one Canadian storytellers from various backgrounds and from across Canada have contributed to this spellbinding collection of stories about love, wisdom and change. "... while [the storytellers] will probably be forgotten, their stories will be remembered." *Quill & Quire*

ISBN 0-921556-46-2 $12.95

The Storyteller at Fault
Dan Yashinsky

A masterful tale of adventure, wit and suspense, by an accomplished raconteur. Folk literature and oral traditions from around the world are woven into a colourful tapestry that is a whole new tale in itself.

ISBN 0-921556-29-2 $9.95

Mogul and Me
Peter Cumming
Illustrated by P. John Burden

Based on a true story, this dramatic tale of the friendship between a New Brunswick farmboy and a circus elephant is also a story of love and trust, and good and evil.

ISBN 0-920304-82-6 $8.95

RAGWEED PRESS books can be found in quality bookstores, or individual orders may be sent prepaid to: RAGWEED PRESS, P.O. Box 2023, Charlottetown, Prince Edward Island, Canada, C1A 7N7. Please add postage and handling ($2.45 for the first book and 75 cents for each additional book) to your order. Canadian residents add 7% GST to the total amount. GST registration number R104383120.